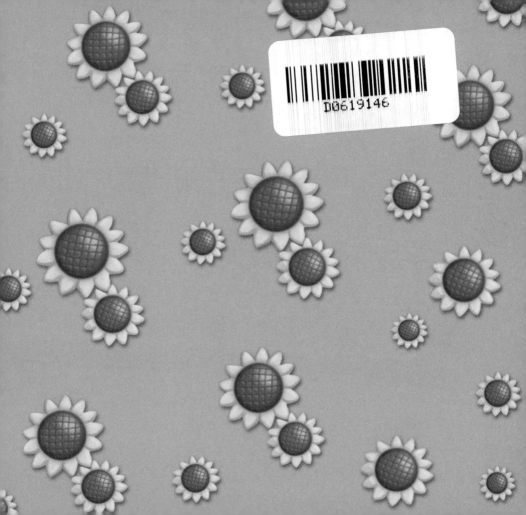

EGMONT

We bring stories to life

First published in Australia and New Zealand 2009
by Egmont UK Limited,
239 Kensington High Street, London W8 6SA
Endpapers and introductory illustrations by Craig Cameron

HiT entertainment

ISBN 978 1 4052 4868 6

3 5 7 9 10 8 6 4 2

Printed in Singapore

Travis
and the Tropical Fruit

Illustrations by Dynamo

EGMONT

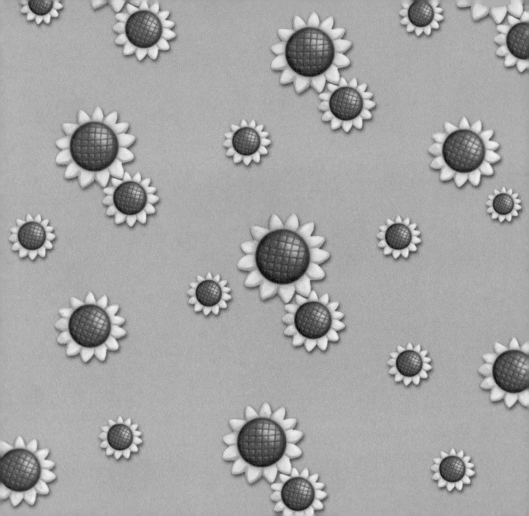

When Mr Beasley says he wants to grow pineapples in Sunflower Valley, Travis offers to help. But things go wrong, and Travis and Spud make a real stink!

Travis the tractor had come to visit his friends in Sunflower Valley.

"Farmer Pickles has gone to Bobsville today," said Travis. "Got any jobs for me?"

"No, sorry, Travis," said Scoop. "But there'll be a job somewhere! You just have to look for it!"

Meanwhile, Mr Beasley was showing a special box to Bob and Wendy.

"My pineapple seedlings have just been delivered!" he smiled, opening the box.

Bob and Wendy were puzzled.

"Sunflower Valley's not hot enough to grow pineapples!" said Bob. "They grow in tropical weather!"

"But the box says they need planting straight away!" Mr Beasley frowned.

"Don't worry," said Wendy, kindly. "Let's look up pineapples on the Internet."

Wendy found a picture of a pineapple pit on her computer and showed Mr Beasley.

"I've never built one of those!" laughed Bob. "It looks like your pineapples are going to be heated by horse manure!"

Bob went to the yard to tell the team.

"What's horse manure?" asked Muck.

"It's, erm, horse poo," said Bob. "It sounds silly, but it will heat up the pineapples and make them grow!"

"I moved a whole load of horse manure at Farmer Pickles' farm yesterday," said Travis. "I'll fetch it and be back before you know it!"

The farm was far away in Bobsville, but Travis got there quickly. He loaded up his trailer with the horse manure.

Just then, his talkie-talkie began to crackle. It was Bob!

"Take your time, Travis," said Bob. "The pineapple pit isn't built yet . . . and manure is a bit smelly!"

"Ha, ha! Erm, OK, Bob," said Travis.

Travis decided to unload the manure in a clearing beside the Bentleys' eco house, until Bob needed it.

Nearby, the Bentleys and the Sabatinis were having a picnic.

"Goodness me! Whatever's that smell?" said Mr Bentley. "We can't stay here. Quick, pack up the picnic!"

"Oh, deary me!" worried Travis, and he trundled away with the trailer of manure.

The next day, Mr Beasley went to see how Bob and the team were getting on. They had been very busy building the pineapple pit.

"When we put the manure in, it will heat up the soil and make the seedlings grow!" Bob told Mr Beasley.

"These glass covers will keep them warm and the pong inside!" Wendy laughed.

Travis had taken his trailer to Scarecrow Cottage. He needed Spud to help him move the manure.

"My parsnip nose! What a whiff!" said Spud. He disappeared inside the cottage and came back wearing a funny mask.

"Ta da! Spud's wearing Farmer Pickles' special mask for cleaning out the pig sties!" boomed Spud, through his mask.

Soon, Spud and Travis had made a plan.

"The big pile of manure makes a big stink, but lots of little piles will just make lots of little stinks," said Spud.

"No one'll notice a thing!" agreed Travis.

So Spud shovelled the manure into sacks, then Travis took them away to hide all over Sunflower Valley.

A few days later, it was time to add the manure to the pineapple pits.

Travis and Spud told Bob about how they had stored it in the sacks. "We hid them all over Sunflower Valley," said Spud.

"Oh, dear!" chuckled Bob. "How will we find them again?"

Just then, Mr Bentley arrived. "Don't worry," he said. "I'll soon sniff them out!"

And that's just what they did! Spud, Travis and Mr Bentley searched behind bushes, trees and buildings until they had found all the sacks.

"Wow!" said Travis. "What a clever nose you have, Mr Bentley!"

They took the sacks to Bob, and he and Spud shovelled the manure into the pits.

Before long, the pineapple pits were as hot as a tropical jungle!

Months passed while the pineapples grew, until finally they were ready to eat.

Mr Beasley invited everyone to taste the tropical treat, and it was delicious!

"Horse manure! That's the secret," he laughed. "I'm going to grow all sorts of tropical fruit next – mangoes, bananas . . ."

"Oh, no! You know what that means, Travis," groaned Bob. "More manure!"

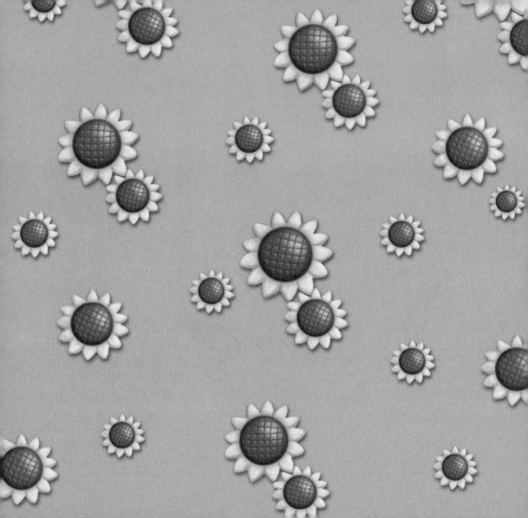

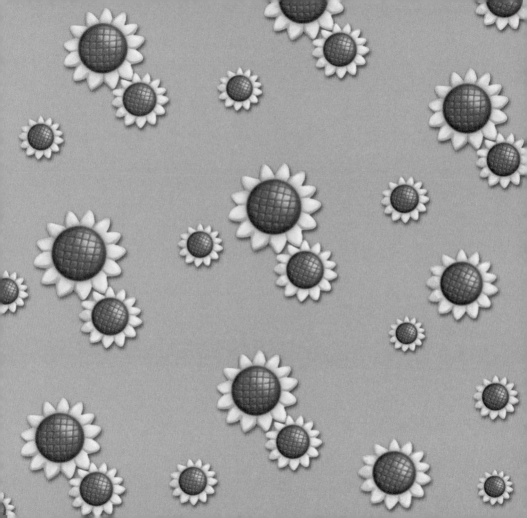